Sins of the Father

A Jaz Blackwell Mystery, Volume 1

Odell Theadford

Published by Odell Theadford, 2024.

SINS OF THE FATHER

First edition. February 8, 2024.

ISBN: 979-8223082743

Written by Odell Theadford.

I am deeply grateful to Dr. Marcia of *Creative Concepts by Dr. Marcia* for her invaluable expertise and guidance in developing the branding and strategy for this book. Her thoughtful insights and wealth of experience were instrumental in clarifying my vision and goals. Thank you, Dr. Marcia, for sharing your knowledge and helping me create a distinctive, memorable identity for my work.

https://creativeconceptsbydrmarcia.com

Prologue

The night air was thick with tension as Ezekiel Blackwell crept along the edge of the shipping yard, squinting through the darkness. He could hear the lap of water against the docks nearby, punctuated by the creak of rigging and occasional shouts from the crew members loading cargo onto an aged steamer ship.

Ezekiel hesitated behind a stack of crates, hand hovering near the revolver on his hip. According to the informant, a major deal was going down tonight between the elusive Serpent's Tail crime syndicate and a group of smugglers they often employed. If he could just get photographic evidence, it would be the break in the case he'd been chasing for years.

Up ahead, the bobbing beam of a flashlight cut through the darkness. Ezekiel shrank back into the shadows, his breath shallow. The light drew nearer, and soon, two armed guards emerged, flanking a man in a fine suit—the notorious crime boss himself.

Ezekiel silently cursed. His vantage point was too distant to get a clear shot. He'd have to get closer. Palming his camera, he crept around cargo containers until he found a spot with a direct line of sight. The crime boss was shaking hands with a smuggler, confirming the exchange. This was his chance.

With a steady hand, Ezekiel raised his camera to snap photos, the flash muted. But suddenly he sensed movement behind him a second too late. A heavy blow struck the back of his head and Ezekiel collapsed, vision blurring. Rough hands dragged him deeper into the maze of cargo.

"Thought you could spy on us, Blackwell?" a menacing voice growled. "You won't be sharing what you saw with anyone."

Ezekiel was thrown against a metal container, hitting it with a sickening crack. Dazed, he tried to fight back but took a savage punch to the gut that left him gasping for air. Blood streaming from his temple, he was forced to his knees.

"Please..." he choked out before a boot connected with his jaw, filling his mouth with the iron taste of blood. More blows rained down as he begged for mercy.

Finally, meaty hands closed around Ezekiel's throat, squeezing relentlessly as his face purpled and vision darkened at the edges. With a last desperate gasp, he choked out "Jaz, Tasha...I'm sorry," before going limp.

His body was heaved into the freezing water without ceremony. The ship's moorings were loosened and set off into the night, taking Ezekiel's hopes of making it home to his family. Justice would have to wait, but Ezekiel clung to faith that one day, the truth he had uncovered would come to light.

Chapter 1

Jaz Blackwell's athletic, imposing 6'2" frame stood confidently behind the carved pulpit at Spirit Song Fellowship. His muscular physique, honed from years of physical training, filled out his well-tailored suit. Jaz gripped the edges of the pulpit as if they were lifelines connecting him to his congregation. His deep-set brown eyes, reflecting a lifetime of struggle and service, scanned the faces before him. Each face told a tale of concealed battles seeking solace within the knit community of this sanctuary. His smooth dark skin and precisely faded haircut gave Jaz an air of refined confidence. Taking a moment to compose himself, hints of a subtle smile playing on his features, he prepared to deliver a sermon that held meaning and personal significance.

"Throughout texts, we often encounter the phrase 'Sins of the Father '" he began, each word carrying weight and filling the room with solemnity. "You see, the Bible addresses how previous generations leave their imprints upon us and how we inherit responsibilities as their successors."

He then turned his attention to a Bible resting on the pulpit's surface. Gently tracing his finger along its pages until he found a passage from Ezekiel, he read aloud with an unwavering conviction in his voice, "The sins of a father shall not burden his son, nor shall a father bear responsibility for sins committed by his child. Everyone shall bear their righteousness or wickedness."

Taking a pause, he allowed the congregation a moment to reflect upon this scripture. "So, what does this mean for us in today's world? What does it mean to grapple with the notion of 'inherited sin', in relation to the obstacles we encounter?" Jaz paced back and forth, his voice brimming with fervor. "Just as some individuals inherit wealth, we also inherit injustices and inequalities that have existed before our time. However, the Bible also teaches us that each person bears their burdens. We all possess the ability to seek redemption."

He made eye contact with his congregation. "You see, the Bible is not only a set of instructions for life; it is a guide that adds complexity to our understanding of it. It impels us to confront systems we have inherited, systems often constructed on falsehoods and biases, while acknowledging our power to pursue justice and truth.

Even Jesus Himself championed justice as a warrior flipping tables when merchants defiled the temple. He could have easily turned an eye claiming those were not His sins. He didn't. He fought for justice. Shouldn't we?" Jaz's voice soared with conviction fueled by his words.

As he wrapped up his sermon, he knew he had touched upon layers that deeply resonated with his congregation. "Therefore, my brothers and sisters let us learn from the mistakes of our forefathers without letting them define our lives. Always keep in mind that anyone can find redemption no matter their circumstances. Embrace the challenges that come your way knowing that you have the ability to shape not only your future but also the future of generations to come."

The audience rose to their feet applauding and expressing their agreement with Amen. They were profoundly spiritually awakened by his words. What they couldn't perceive was the sense of urgency in Jaz's sermon. He wasn't just speaking to them; he was also speaking to himself as he grappled with his legacy. The mysterious disappearance of his father and the unanswered questions it brought into his life weighed heavily on him. As Jaz stepped away from the pulpit, a mix of determination and bewilderment swirled within him knowing that soon these words would be put to the test.

As the parishioners exited the church one by one Jaz stood by the doorway exchanging handshakes and pleasantries. Usually, he would stay longer on Sundays to answer questions or offer guidance. However, today a sense of urgency urged him forward. When he was at home in his study, he checked the mail from yesterday. His heart raced when he noticed an envelope without a return address or recipient label. With trembling hands, he tore it open.

Jaz skimmed through the letter his brow furrowing, in confusion. On the surface its contents seemed harmless—a reminiscence of childhood memories of fishing with his father.

Every sentence contained chosen phrases that hinted at the answers he had been searching for,

over three decades. These answers revolved around his father's disappearance, which occurred just as he was closing in on a ruthless crime syndicate.

Phrases like "the grass on the bank of the eastern side" and "his hand tightened before the line went slack" served as clues. They referred to details that only someone intimately involved in the case would be aware of.

As Jaz read through these crafted sentences, he could feel a tremor in his hands as hidden meanings began to unravel. The anonymous letter writer claimed to possess insider information about what happened to his father.

Within the language lay an offer—a chance to finally uncover the truth in exchange for assistance in bringing down the individuals who remained at large within the syndicate. It was an opportunity for justice to be served and for those responsible for his father's death—individuals—to be captured.

A cold sensation ran down Jaz's brow as tiny droplets of sweat formed, a reaction to hearing words he had longed for over years; "I know what happened to your father. I know the truth."

Jaz paced restlessly in his study, feeling his heart thump as he debated whether to share the letter with his sister, Tasha. After enduring minutes, he ultimately concluded that it was crucial for her to be informed, particularly considering the potential dangers associated with this investigation.

He made his way to the kitchen where Tasha was preparing Sunday dinner. Trying to appear nonchalant, he casually mentioned receiving a piece of mail related to their father's disappearance. He handed her the letter with an air of indifference.

Initially, Tasha's face displayed confusion as she attempted to decipher the metaphors and hidden meanings within. As realization slowly dawned upon her, her hands began trembling. "Oh, my goodness," she whispered in disbelief. "This individual claims to possess knowledge about Dad's disappearance."

Jaz nodded solemnly. "I understand that it is most likely a prank. On the chance that it holds any truth. "He didn't need to finish his sentence; the yearning to finally unravel their father's disappearance weighed heavily in their minds.

Tasha's eyes filled with gleam as she reminisced about memories from family fishing trips and recalled her father's hearty laughter bedtime stories shared, and playful teasing moments. Though she was five years old when he vanished into the air, fragments of those precious moments remained etched in her memory. His absence had created a wound that still caused pain decades later.

Tears welled up in Tasha's eyes as she leaned against the sturdy granite countertop. After a moment she spoke with unwavering conviction. "Jaz, it's crucial that you pursue this. We can't be sure if another chance for answers will come our way."

Jaz ran his fingers through his hair torn between emotions. "It's risky, Tasha. What if it puts everything we've built in jeopardy? The church, our family." His voice trailed off as he thought about his niece.

Tasha walked across the kitchen and firmly grasped Jaz's arm. "Listen to me carefully. Our family was forever changed when Daddy disappeared. We managed to survive, but there is still an emptiness within us. You became a police officer because you wanted justice. If there's a possibility of uncovering the truth, you owe it to yourself to pursue it."

With a swallow, Jaz finally nodded in agreement. She was right; he couldn't ignore this, no matter how risky it seemed.

Sensing his consent, Tasha spoke more resolutely. "I'll take care of Lisa and make sure everything runs smoothly at the church. You need to focus on unraveling this mystery." A faint smile played on her lips.

Jaz chuckled as the grip of anxiety on his chest loosened slightly. His sister had a knack for putting things into perspective. With her approval, he felt prepared to chase after this lead no matter where it led him.

That night, after Tasha and Lisa had departed, Jaz found himself alone again, carefully examining the encoded letter. Doubt still lingered within him. He could not disregard his responsibility to their father and the young boy who had suddenly lost him.

Jaz whispered a prayer for guidance before retrieving his gun from the safe in his closet. After checking the magazine, he committed himself to the investigation. If this lead revealed a fraction of the truth, he was determined to delve into the darkness. It was not only for his father's sake but also for Tasha and himself—a wounded soul still searching for solace.

Chapter 2

The following morning Jaz made a stop at the county morgue to meet up with his friend Marcus.

Restlessly pacing back and forth as Marcus scrutinized the letter using forensic tools it felt like an eternity before Marcus finally looked up with a gleam in his eye.

"Clearly whoever wrote this took every precaution. There aren't any marks or smudges on the outside of the envelope. Marcus pointed out a spot in the corner of the letter where he managed to collect a partial thumbprint.

He beckoned Jaz over to look at the sample under the microscope. Although not an expert Jaz could vaguely make out the swirls and ridges. Marcus explained how this could be a clue.

With excitement building, Marcus swiftly entered the fingerprint into the database by typing commands on the keyboard. As thousands of fingerprints were scanned for a match, Jaz struggled to remain calm.

Finally, there was a sound indicating success, and Marcus exclaimed, "We've got a match!" He tilted the screen so that Jaz could see it. The name Joseph Duncan appeared along with his record. Jaz's eyes widened as he absorbed the magnitude of Duncan's several-decade history.

"Armed robbery, assault, involvement in racketeering activities suspected ties to organized crime." Marcus listed off. "This guy is trouble. I believe he's either an enforcer or a hired gun, for one of our syndicates. If he's behind this, it would explain all this coded language and secrecy." Jaz experienced a mix of hope and fear as he absorbed the information. It was a game-changer. Duncan's mysterious background seemed to align with someone who had knowledge about Jaz's father's case.

Marcus placed a hand on Jaz's shoulder, understanding the weight of this revelation. "We'll get to the bottom of this, don't worry. I'll delve deeper into Duncan's connections and criminal activities."

Jaz nodded, finding support by steadying himself against the examination table while memories flooded his mind. He recalled his father meticulously tying his tie every morning before heading to the police station, always inspiring his fellow detectives with his unwavering determination. He remembered those fishing trips when his father patiently taught him how to bait a hook.

Then everything changed, the void, the empty casket, and countless unanswered questions. Jaz made a promise to uncover every detail of Duncan's life to unravel the mystery surrounding his father's disappearance.

Within this place surrounded by death, that single piece of evidence brought more vitality than Jaz had felt in years. The possibility of finding closure by honoring his father's memory and acknowledging his noble sacrifice fueled Jaz's determination.

Overwhelmed with gratitude, Jaz embraced Marcus tightly, the bond between them strengthened by their shared care and support of one another. Then he straightened his posture and walked out with determination ready to continue his pursuit of truth and justice. With Marcus' expertise in forensics and his own determination, he would follow the trail that his father abruptly left behind years ago.

For the sake of both his father and him, Jaz embraced the path that lay ahead. The ghosts of the past could no longer remain hidden. He was determined to confront them. He wouldn't stop until the complete truth finally came to light after being denied for too long.

Stepping out of the morgue into the night air Jaz exhaled, watching as his breath formed wispy clouds while Marcus' revelation echoed in his mind.

Joseph Duncan.

Just hearing that name seemed to awaken shadows calling forth buried secrets. This ruthless enforcer deeply embedded in the underworld might hold the key to unraveling the mystery surrounding his father's fate.

Leaning against the cold brick wall, Jaz flooded with memories. He remembered the times they had gone fishing together, his father lifting him up whenever they caught something. He played cops and robbers around their home, with his father assigning roles and promising they would be partners against crime. He assisted his father in polishing his detective badge until it shone, envisioning the day he would earn one of his own.

Then came the overwhelming absence. His mother cried when they received the call that his father had disappeared while chasing after an organization. He visited his father's desk avoiding the gazes as he touched the nameplate and badge. The somber finality of the funeral, holding his sister's hand as they lowered the empty casket into the ground. A life extinguished without explanation leaving a void in their family.

Over the years that followed Jaz channeled his pain into following in his father's footsteps, even taking a copy of his case file with him when he left the police force. He held onto hope that someday everything would align perfectly, and through determination, he would uncover the answers that had eluded him for decades.

Now, a tangible lead had emerged—one that could unravel the veil hiding the circumstances surrounding his father's death. Jaz closed his eyes, picturing his father's approving smile and determined nod. The years of stillness burst into action again. The hunt resumed.

As Jaz pushed away from the wall, he felt a renewed sense of purpose coursing through him.

He planned to utilize his connections, in the streets and within law enforcement, reaching out to every favor and utilizing all resources to locate Duncan. He was determined to pursue every lead connected to the organization that caused his father's demise regardless of how high up the hierarchy it led. .

In that moment Jaz felt a sense of harmony in the universe as if the winds of change were on his side. Looking up at the night sky he softly murmured, "This is it, Dad. I'll finally make things right." A shooting star streaked across the sky almost as if his father watched over him and guided him on this path towards justice.

With renewed energy, Jaz ventured into the darkness. He embraced the risks and enigma that awaited him. His father's legacy echoed through time. He vowed not to rest until he had responded to its call. The pursuit had begun.

Chapter 3

Jaz and Mia, former partners in the homicide department, sat together at a diner. Even though Jaz had left the police force years ago their bond remained strong. Mia was always there for him when investigating his father's case.

"Hey Jaz, long time no see," Mia warmly greeted him, her observant eyes narrowing slightly as she noticed his demeanor. After exchanging pleasantries, Jaz shared the details of a letter that seemed to be linked to his dad.

Taking a breath, Mia immediately grasped the seriousness of the situation. She remembered how consumed Jaz had been with unraveling the mystery of his father's fate, nights spent going through files and following leads that led nowhere. She knew this recent breakthrough would bring back memories while also opening possibilities.

Leaning in closer, Jaz locked eyes with Mia. "I know it's a risky request. I need your help accessing those case files. My father was getting close to exposing the syndicate before they silenced him. If there are any leads or clues hidden in those files, we need to uncover them."

Expecting some resistance, Jaz was pleasantly surprised when Mia nodded in agreement. The bond they had developed over their years of duty created a sense of trust between them. She understood how important it was for Jaz to solve this case. Her unwavering dedication to justice fueled her determination to bring these insiders to account.

"I'll gather all the documents. Then we can meet at your place tomorrow evening," Mia assured him. While her superiors dismissed it as another forgotten case, she saw it as an opportunity to find closure.

Jaz felt a weight lifted off his shoulders and breathed a sigh of relief. He knew Mia's sharp intellect and fearless instincts would make her an invaluable partner in this mission. With Marcus' expertise in forensics and Mia having his back on the streets, he allowed himself to feel a glimmer of hope.

They spent some time there conversing while reminiscing about their shared experiences during patrols.

Despite their career paths, they seamlessly worked together, with their abilities complementing one another perfectly. With Mia's assistance, Jaz felt a surge of confidence, knowing he could continue where his father left off abruptly thirty years ago.

They bid farewell, setting a time to meet tomorrow. He felt deeply touched by Mia's support in his quest to unravel the mysteries of the past. She had become his ally in his quest. She handed him a valuable tool: loyalty. With her assistance, the hidden truths concealed within those case files would finally be revealed.

The records room was deathly silent, the only light came from the moon through the barred windows. Mia's pulse thundered as she unsteadily hand-picked the lock. Finally, the latch clicked, the sound echoing ominously.

Mia's pulse quickened as she slipped into the deserted records room past midnight. Finding the cold case archives, she quickly located the box labeled "Det. Blackwell." Trembling, Mia lifted the lid and rifled through the faded folders within.

This was a risky maneuver, even for her. If the chief found out she had accessed these confidential records without authorization, it could cost her badge. But the truth mattered more.

Mia snapped photos of key documents on her phone—conflicting eyewitness reports, suspicious transfers, and resignations. She hesitated over the original detective's logbook—it would be invaluable to Jaz but also impossible to conceal.

Footsteps in the hall sent her heart lurching. Hastily returning the other files, she stashed the logbook at the bottom of the box and resealed it. The steps passed by.

Knowing time was running out, Mia lifted the heavy box and cracked the door. The halls were still clear. Keeping to the shadows, she crept towards the rear exit.

Almost there. Mia shifted the awkward box, wiping sweat from her eyes. Suddenly, a door opened, and she ducked behind a pillar, throat clenched.

After an agonizing minute, she continued, finally easing the door open. Melting into the concealing darkness outside, Mia inhaled shakily. Phase one was complete. Now, we need to decode what secrets are awaited within those files.

Adrenaline was still pumping as she loaded her cargo into the trunk, mind racing ahead to the next perilous steps in exposing the buried truth.

As the evening progressed, Jaz's excitement grew. He eagerly awaited Mia's arrival. A surge of anticipation coursed through him, intensifying his burning desire to uncover the truth. Suddenly, the sound of Mia's car pulling up shattered the silence of the night. Without hesitation, Jaz hurried towards her vehicle with a sense of urgency pulsating in his heart.

"Did you manage to get hold of the files?" he asked urgently, his voice brimming with anticipation.

In response, Mia gestured to him to check the trunk. She popped it open. Taking a breath, Jaz focused his gaze on a weathered cardboard box. The name DET. BLACKWELL was roughly scribbled across its side – sending shivers down his spine. Inside lay his father's case files – a treasure trove that awaited answers.

"I quickly skimmed through them, " Mia shared as they made their way towards the house, curiosity filling her voice. "The initial investigation was chaotic. The reports are filled with contradictions that cast doubt on what happened before your father mysteriously vanished."

A sense of unease tugged at Jaz, urging him to delve into this web of accounts. According to the lead detective's report, Jaz's father appeared to have reached a dead end in his investigation before vanishing. A junior officer's account painted a different picture. It portrayed his father as a determined man on the verge of making a significant breakthrough in the case.

Jaz's hand trembled slightly as he focused on his father's written notes on each page. These words revealed a story that unfolded like a tapestry, exposing a planned meeting with an informant who possessed incriminating evidence against the organization's leader. This rendezvous was scheduled to take place on the day Jaz's father disappeared without a trace.

"I believe this proves that my dad uncovered something that may have led to his demise," Jaz whispered. Mia nodded solemnly in agreement.

While going through the files, Jaz stumbled upon a document ordering the transfer of the lead detective two days after his father went missing. The timing immediately raised suspicions.

"It appears they manipulated things to remove that detective from the case when things got complicated," Mia remarked. "Then he used his influence to conceal what truly happened."

A shiver ran down Jaz's spine as all the puzzle pieces finally fell into place. His father had been forever silenced when he was about to reveal the syndicate's leader. It seemed that someone in a high position deliberately concealed the truth.

There was still a glimmer of hope of finding out where the informant was hiding. Jaz knew that Mia had resources to track down aliases and investigate their methods, which could help locate him. Meanwhile, Jaz planned to apply pressure on his contacts within the department to inquire about the detective's transfer.

As they continued discussing the case, Jaz felt a sense of relief, and uncertainty began to dissipate. The impenetrable silence surrounding his father's situation started cracking, showing signs of optimism. The informant and emerging "evidence" are now essential parts of this intricate puzzle.

"I am determined to unravel this," Jaz confided to Mia in a sure tone. The circumstances surrounding his father's case had transcended beyond being another missing person report. This presented an opportunity for them to uncover the truth and achieve justice, something that often seemed elusive within a law enforcement agency entrusted with upholding it.

In the weeks that followed, Jaz and Mia tirelessly pursued leads in their quest to unveil the informant's identity while also exerting pressure to gather information about why the lead detective was suspiciously removed from the investigation. Their unwavering persistence eventually paid off.

Through informants and various connections, Mia discovered that Tomas Suarez, a player involved in illegal gambling with extensive underworld ties, had been the one providing Jaz's father with information. Jaz's sources revealed that influential individuals higher up than their Chief had orchestrated the detective's transfer.

Chapter 4

Suarez nursed his beer in the shadowy corner of the bar, keeping his head down. It's been 12 years since Detective Blackwell disappeared. He's been living off the grid in Grand Junction, Colorado. He believed there was no further risk in returning to Charleston for a quick visit. So far, he had avoided notice.

Leaving the bar and ducking into the shadows, Suarez hurried down the familiar streets he had known as home, saying silent goodbyes. Maybe someday, he could return without fear. But not while Blackwell's case remained unsolved.

Suarez staggered through the alley, constantly glancing behind him with unease. Ever since he had uncovered the syndicate's incriminating secrets, he had felt he was being watched while in Charleston. He regretted coming back. "I should have never come back. It was good to see the family, but it is time to get out of here," he whispered to himself.

He wished he had followed his original thoughts many years ago when his sole objective was to reach the police station and hand over the evidence, ensuring his entry into witness protection as promised.

With a pounding heart, Suarez maneuvered through a gap in the chain link fence that bordered the railway yard. Suddenly, a black sedan screeched to a halt before him, effectively blocking his escape route. Suarez spun around in panic only to find himself confronted by two towering figures whose faces were concealed by shadows.

"Please," Suarez pleaded desperately, "there's no need for this! I'll give you anything you want!"

One of the men delivered a punch to his stomach, causing Suarez to double over in pain. They forcefully slammed him against the sedan. Immobilized his arms. Despite his struggle, their grip seemed unyielding.

One man held a cloth soaked in chloroform against Suarez's face, rendering him unconscious, with muffled screams gradually fading away.

The other swiftly bound his hands and feet before he succumbed completely.

When Suarez regained consciousness, he found himself confined to a chair within a cabin.

He struggled against the ropes in vain as a man prepared a syringe.

"Who sent you? What are you after?" Suarez croaked, his throat dry.

The man smirked coldly, flicking the needle. "Sorry, pal. Just taking care of some loose ends."

He jabbed the needle into Suarez's arm and depressed the plunger, sending potassium chloride and other chemicals coursing through his veins.

Suarez thrashed violently against his bonds as his heart began palpitating erratically. Unable to clutch his chest, he screamed in agony before collapsing forward.

The man watched impassively as Suarez convulsed in cardiac distress, his heart muscle destroyed by the injected toxins. With a final weak shudder, Suarez went still, eyes glassy and lifeless.

The corrupt medical examiner would label it a convenient "heart attack." The truth would die alongside Suarez in that remote cabin.

Piece by piece, Jaz and Mia slowly unraveled the puzzle, fueling their determination further. The price they paid for seeking the truth had been painfully high. They felt compelled to ensure that both his father and Suarez didn't die in vain. The secrets they sacrificed for could still be revealed if Jaz and Mia remained resolute.

Committed to their cause, they promised to unravel this web undeterred by the potential dangers involved. They were determined not to rest until genuine justice was served.

Tomas Suarez and his father had passed away years ago under suspicious circumstances. Jaz knew he had to dig and investigate. He decided to approach Marcus for assistance.

When Jaz met Marcus at the morgue, he sensed a seriousness in the demeanor of his usual light-hearted friend.

Marcus, rubbing his head, said, "I was able to find Suarez's autopsy report in the database."

Together, they carefully examined Suarez's report, and Marcus drew attention to the cause of death: an infarction or heart attack at the age of 42. "Seems straightforward," he skeptically remarked.

Jaz felt frustration building up inside him as he clenched his jaw. "We both know there's more to it than that. Please elaborate on your observations."

Jaz leaned in as Marcus indicated faint bruising on Suarez's wrists and ankles. "Ligature marks," he said grimly. Consistent with being forcibly restrained."

Tracing the ugly purpling on Suarez's chest, Marcus explained, "Blunt force trauma, like he violently struggled against his captor." Jaz winced at the thought.

Marcus then produced close-ups of Suarez's bloodshot eyes. "See these ruptured capillaries? A classic indicator of cardiac arrest." He went on, "But it's these small injection marks that tell the real story."

He directed Jaz's attention to barely perceptible puncture wounds dotting Suarez's arms. "Toxicology showed only 'therapeutic' sedative levels. But based on the other anomalies, these were injections to trigger a fatal heart attack."

Marcus sat back, letting the disturbing conclusions sink in. "They chemically induced cardiac arrest to mimic natural causes. But the ligature marks, petechiae, and trauma tell a darker tale - homicide staged as a natural death."

Jaz scrubbed a hand down his face, anger and frustration swirling. The cover-up surrounding Suarez's murder ran even more profound than expected. But Marcus's keen eye helped reveal the truth.

Marcus leaned back in his chair to allow his findings to sink in. Jaz ran his hand over his mouth, his mind racing with thoughts. "They silenced Suarez by killing him. Made it appear natural. Like what happened to my father when they made it look like he abandoned our family," Jaz murmured as his voice trailed off.

"You're right," Marcus agreed grimly. "The cardiac arrest itself could seem natural, but with the restraint marks, blunt force trauma, and injection sites...this has 'homicide staged as a heart attack' written all over it."

He shook his head, anger flashing in his eyes. "Suarez must have discovered something big, something worth killing over. They chemically induced a heart attack to cover their tracks."

Jaz braced his hands on the cold exam table to steady himself. Marcus was right - the gaps were coming together to form a sinister picture. Suarez had been brutally silenced just like his father, their secrets dying alongside them.

But he and Marcus would keep digging until the dark web of deception came to light. Justice would be served, no matter how high the cost. With his friend's keen insight and determination, Jaz felt hopeful they could unravel the sinister staged death. The truth had to prevail.

Marcus placed a hand on his friend's shoulder. "I understand how tough this situation is. Your dad and Suarez left us with a trail to follow. We'll make sure it carries meaning."

Jaz's face hardened with determination. Marcus was right. Suarez had paid the price while trying to gather evidence against the syndicate. They owed it to him and Jaz's father to see this mission through.

Taking a breath, Jaz continued, "Alright. Our next move is to uncover Suarez's evidence about the leader. Maybe there are some details in my dad's case files or even in Suarez's belongings..."

Marcus nodded, his eyes gleaming with familiarity and anticipation of seeking the truth. "I'll reach out to some trusted colleagues in pathology. Ask if they notice any elements in the reports that can further establish foul play."

A sense of gratitude washed over Jaz as he realized how lucky he was to have Marcus by his side, someone with expertise and unwavering dedication. Together, they were determined to unravel the web of deception surrounding these deaths that had been hidden for too long. Finally, those buried secrets would get an opportunity to come into the light.

As Jaz and Marcus walked out of the morgue, a strange feeling washed over Jaz, almost as if his father's presence was urging him to act. The price they had paid to pursue justice had been extremely high. They were determined not to let the sacrifices made go to waste.

Chapter 5

Restlessly drumming his fingers on the worn-out table in the corner of the security office, Jaz anxiously awaited any news about his niece, Lisa. He had received a call from the department store informing him that she had been caught shoplifting.

After what felt like an eternity, the door swung open. A security guard brought in a dejected Lisa. Taking note of her torn jeans, hoodie, and glimpses of blonde hair peeking out from under her beanie, Jaz observed how she avoided eye contact as she slumped down on the chair across from him.

"This one got caught trying to stuff makeup into her bag," grumbled the guard. "We're giving her a warning this time since it's her first offense. If it happens again, she'll be taken into custody and charged."

Jaz nodded calmly while maintaining a composed expression until the guard left. Then he locked eyes with Lisa and asked sternly, "What were you thinking? Seriously?"

Lisa shrugged defiantly while glaring at the table. "It's not such a big deal. I was trying out some new styles."

"It's quite a big deal," Jaz replied firmly. "Do you realize the impact that getting arrested could have on your future?"

Lisa responded dismissively, rolling her eyes. "Oh, please. All you have to do is make a phone call, and they'll erase it from my record. That's what people like you do."

Her casual remark triggered Jaz's anger. He snapped back, "It's not that simple! I won't always be there to fix your messes. There are consequences."

"Don't be ridiculous," Lisa scoffed. "Guys like you never face the consequences." She pushed herself away from the table. Impatiently asked, "Can we leave already?"

Taking a breath, Jaz tried to remain composed: "Give me a moment to speak with them? ... Stay here."

He stepped out. He talked with the head of security, explaining Lisa's family situation and ensuring they would get her help. After more conversation, the man agreed not to file a report this time.

When Jaz returned, Lisa appeared surprised. She quickly resumed her sulky demeanor. They rode home in silence. As Lisa made a move to hastily exit the car, Jaz called out, "We need to have a conversation about this."

"There's nothing left to say! Oh my God!" she exclaimed, walking angrily towards the house.

Jaz followed her inside. Tasha had already been informed by a call from the store. When Tasha found out that Jaz had intervened, anger flashed in her eyes.

"You can't keep shielding her from the consequences! She'll never learn." Tasha seethed. Lisa shouted that nobody understood her and disappeared into her room.

Jaz ran his hands down his face, feeling shame wash over him. Tasha was right – Lisa was heading down the wrong path, and he was only enabling her.

Jaz was sitting on the sofa in the living room reading a file. Lisa stood at the doorway looking uncertain. "I'm sorry for saying that you never face consequences," she said softly. "I know it's not true."

Jaz gestured for Lisa to sit beside him on the couch. She took a breath, her voice trembling as she whispered, "I miss my dad. It hurts every day he's not here."

In a gesture, Jaz wrapped his arm around Lisa's shoulders. He knew firsthand the pain of missing a father.

"I understand how difficult it is for your dad to be on deployment," he said gently. "Always remember that he is serving our country with honor and loves you deeply."

Lisa nodded, brushing away a tear. "I know. I'm proud of him. It's just so tough to be away from him. The house feels so empty without him." She leaned her head against Jaz's shoulder.

"You're not alone, my dear. We're family and support one another," Jaz assured her warmly. "I can never replace your father. I'll always be here for you whenever you need me."

Lisa managed a grateful smile in response. Jaz's unwavering presence provided solace when she felt lost and longed for her deployed father. Together, they found comfort in the understanding they shared.

Jaz wrapped an arm around her shoulders, feeling his grief well up inside him. "I understand," he said softly. "We're going to make it through this." They found solace in each other's presence, finding strength despite their shared grief.

Chapter 6

Mia took a breath. Firmly knocked on the door labeled "Police Chief Reynolds." She had exhausted all channels in her attempts to reopen Jaz's father's case but had encountered one dead end after another. It was time for a confrontation that would undoubtedly be intense and heated.

"Come in!" called out the Chief. Mia entered the room. Stood at attention. Chief Reynolds glanced up from his paperwork, surprise crossing his weathered face.

"What brings you here, Detective Sanchez?" he asked sarcastically.

Mia held her ground. "I'm formally requesting the reopening of the disappearance case of Detective Blackwell."

The Chief shook his head. "We've been through this before. It is a case that hasn't been pursued in over ten years. I can't allocate resources to chase after ghosts."

Anger surged through Mia. "With all due respect, sir, I firmly believe crucial evidence has been overlooked. Detective Blackwell was on the verge of a breakthrough before he disappeared."

Chief Reynolds scoffed, dismissing it as speculation. "The lead detectives report clearly stated that it was a dead end, nothing."

Mia leaned forward, her voice earnest, "That report was incomplete at best and possibly falsified. The officer's accounts contradict the facts indicating that Detective Blackwell had stumbled upon something."

The Chief's eyes narrowed with intensity. "Be careful with your accusations, Sanchez. You have no evidence to suggest that his report was inaccurate. Questioning the integrity of your superior is crossing the line."

Mia clenched her jaw. Remained determined. "Then allow me to pursue the truth, sir! If there's a chance that more could have been done, we owe it to the Blackwell family and one of our own."

The Chief rose from his desk, face reddening. "You are way out of your lane, Sanchez! I am denying your request, end of discussion. You will be suspended if I hear more of this talk about accusations against fellow officers. Are we clear?"

Mia hesitated, rage boiling up inside her. Justice was so close if only this obstinate man would open his eyes, she thought! She opened her mouth to continue arguing, then stopped herself. She would make no progress this way as much as it infuriated her.

Taking a deep breath, she responded. "Crystal clear, sir. My apologies for overstepping." The words tasted bitter, but she managed to get them out.

Seemingly appeased, the Chief dismissed her with a wave of his hand. Mia walked stiffly from his office, making it around the corner before punching the concrete wall in frustration.

That night, she met Jaz at O'Malley's. "The Chief refused," she fumed, recounting the heated exchange. "But I am not giving up. We will dig into this on our own time if we must."

Jaz nodded, determination etched across his features. "You are right. We do this off the books. We owe it to my father to follow every lead, no matter what the department brass says."

Their eyes met in shared understanding. The truth was hidden in the shadows and the powers wanted it to remain there. But Jaz and Mia would keep hunting and searching for the missing pieces. Justice did not always come through proper channels. Sometimes, you had to blaze your own path.

Chapter 7

Jaz's cell phone suddenly rang, piercing the darkness before dawn. He groped for it, squinting at the clock display. It was 3 a.m. With a racing heart, he answered briskly.

"Hey Jaz! It's Marcus. We've got a bit of a situation. You need to come down to the morgue right away!"

Jaz sat up abruptly, his pulse quickening. "Hold on, slow down. What's happening?"

Marcus sounded tense. "I can't go into details over the phone. Just make your way as fast as possible!" The call ended abruptly.

Adrenaline surged through Jaz's veins as he hastily dressed and hurried to his car. As he sped through the streets towards the morgue, thoughts swirled in his mind.

The Gothic Revival building that housed the morgue soon came into view. Marcus stood inside, pacing back and forth with a stern expression. Without saying a word, he motioned for Jaz to follow him through hallways and into the chilling basement chamber filled with vaults for the deceased.

Marcus pointed towards one drawer labeled 'Duncan, J.' Marcus pulled open the drawer with a metallic scrape that echoed in the heavy silence before him lay what remained of the man whose print was on the letter.

Jaz stared down at Duncan's lifeless body, taking in the lurid bruises encircling his throat. "Strangulation marks," Marcus noted grimly. "And deep too - the killer used tremendous force."

Marcus traced the contusions with a gloved hand. "No hesitation wounds or defensive bruising either. This was an experienced assassin."

He indicated petechiae dots in the eyes. "See these ruptured capillaries? Confirms the cause of death as asphyxiation."

Marcus then turned Duncan's head gently to reveal a precise break in the hyoid bone. "This fracture occurs in about one-third of strangulation victims. It's an unambiguous sign of homicidal violence."

Jaz shook his head, mixed anger and unease swirling within him. "They went to great lengths to silence him. Suffocating with that level of brute power..." He shuddered at the thought.

"It was a clear execution," Marcus agreed. "No effort to make it seem accidental like with Suarez. They wanted to send a message - threaten the syndicate and pay with your life."

Jaz's hands clenched at his sides. "Well, they messed with the wrong man this time. Duncan helped set me on this path, and I aim to finish what he started."

Marcus firmly gripped Jaz's shoulder. "We won't let his death be meaningless. He uncovered the truth. Now it's up to us to reveal it."

Jaz nodded, his father's spirit urging him on. The enemy's ruthless methods only emboldened his own determination to bring justice to the light.

The next morning, Jaz sought solace at Spirit Song Fellowship where he found comfort within its sanctuary. Kneeling in a pew he closed his eyes and offered prayers for guidance.

A gentle voice interrupted his meditation.

Jaz tensed as Alessandra Moretti strode towards him, her piercing green eyes hinting at the formidable intellect within. As one of the top prosecutors in the city, she had crossed paths with Jaz many times before.

"Pastor Blackwell, glad I caught you," she began, flashing a polite but calculated smile. "I have a mutually beneficial proposition I think you'll find intriguing."

Jaz cocked his head warily. "Go on..."

"As you know, I'm prosecuting a very high-profile case against a suspected kingpin with connections throughout this city." She lowered her voice. "I believe, you have valuable insights into his network that could bolster my case."

Crossing his arms, Jaz replied evenly, "And if I did possess such insights, what makes you think I would share them?"

Alessandra's eyes glinted cannily. "Because uncovering the truth means as much to you as it does to me. Our methods may differ, but our end goal is the same."

When Jaz didn't immediately reply, she pressed on. "Help me, and in return, I can provide you access to records and informants relevant to your...extracurricular interests."

Jaz wavered, temptation warring with reluctance. Alessandra sensed his hesitation. "Think of it this way - sometimes we must wade through shades of gray to illuminate the clear, bold lines of truth and justice."

After an agonizing pause, Jaz finally nodded stiffly. Satisfied, Alessandra gave his arm a familiar squeeze. "I'll be in touch. With your insights, we may change this city's very foundations."

As Alessandra's sharp stilettos clicked away, Jaz took a tense breath. Her cunning made her dangerous, but she was undeniably an ally, for now, on the jagged path towards justice. Wary but resolved, he would proceed, illuminating her blind spots when necessary and letting her sharp intellect cut through his own shadows in turn.

Meanwhile, Mia sat in the chief's office as he angrily confronted her. "Staking out police officers? Have you lost your mind, Sanchez?"

Mia stood her ground confidently. "Respectfully, sir, I have evidence indicating that the former detective was receiving payments from the syndicate. He intentionally hindered the investigations into Suarez and Jaz's father."

The chief frowned. "That's an accusation against a veteran detective. Do you have evidence? Is this just another personal vendetta?"

Mia felt irritated but maintained a calm tone. "Whether we have proof or not, it is essential to reexamine the cases he handled in the pursuit of justice. An innocent man was killed, and we failed to take any action!"

The chief glared and increased the volume of his voice. "Your passion for this matter is clouding your judgment. I'm refusing to authorize an investigation. Do not exceed your authority again."

After the meeting, Mia seethed in her car. How could the chief turn a blind eye to corruption within his own team? She knew that righteous anger alone wouldn't win this battle. With patience, the truth still had a chance to prevail.

Jaz hesitated outside the courtroom, feeling uneasy about testifying on behalf of Alessandra as she prosecuted a suspected crime boss. He had reservations about omitting facts to strengthen her case as it seemed like a compromise he wasn't comfortable with.

Alessandra appeared, her sharp green eyes revealing a touch of impatience. "Are you ready for your moment, Pastor Blackwell? This testimony could be crucial."

Jaz shifted uncomfortably, torn between his conflicting thoughts." Are you sure that bending the truth is necessary for justice?"

"There are times when we need to be flexible in our methods," Alessandra replied briskly. "I'm counting on you."

Suppressing his doubts, Jaz took the stand. With Alessandra's questioning, he emphasized the defendant's history while carefully leaving out his own incriminating findings. The blurred lines between truth and falsehood left Jaz unsettled.

Alessandra seemed satisfied with the outcome. The defense team regarded Jaz with suspicion since they knew he hadn't told the entire truth. Under their scrutiny, his conscience wrestled with guilt. Had he compromised his principles?

Afterward, Alessandra expressed gratitude to Jaz for his "skillful" testimony. "With your assistance, we'll permanently bring this criminal to justice."

Jaz forced a smile, feeling hollow inside.

"The pursuit of justice is important. There are always costs involved." Alessandra gently placed her hand on his shoulder. "Sometimes the path of righteousness can lead us into murky territory. The ultimate goal makes it all worth it."

Jaz felt uneasy about Alessandra's sense of right and wrong as they bid each other farewell outside the courthouse. Despite his intentions, the little lies he told still felt like betraying his soul. The righteous outcome hardly seemed to justify his actions.

That night, Jaz shared his doubts with Marcus as they aimlessly strolled through downtown streets.

Marcus listened solemnly before replying. "Moral complexity challenges the foundation. Your character is proven by facing that challenge with courage and compassion. Stay true to your principles no matter how difficult it may be."

Jaz nodded, comforted by his friend's unwavering wisdom. "It's tough to maintain my compass amidst all this deceit. As you said, I need to stay grounded."

"Yeah, that's right. Don't lose yourself chasing after things that don't matter," Marcus said, giving his shoulder a pat. "Remember that deployment in Afghanistan? Grueling desert terrain, but we got through it together," Marcus said, a nostalgic smile crossing his face.

Jaz chuckled, the memory vividly in his mind. "Oh man, I'll never forget that. Endless days marching in full combat gear. We were quite a pair of hardened soldiers back then."

Their laughter momentarily lifted the somber atmosphere. "We looked out for each other, like the time you pulled me to safety when our platoon got ambushed. I trusted you with my life out there," Jaz said.

Marcus nodded solemnly. "We formed an unbreakable bond serving side by side in the sand and heat." He clasped Jaz's shoulder. "Just like now, navigating life's tricky terrain after the war."

Jaz felt a swell of gratitude for this steadfast friend who had walked with him through literal and figurative battlefields. Their shared past forever linked them.

Across town, Mia sat alone in thought, surrounded by case files and a cup of coffee. She was grappling with her crisis of conscience, struggling to find the balance between bending rules for justice and staying true to her values. How far could she compromise before losing sight of what she believed in?

In the station, Mia let out a sigh. Sometimes, upholding truth felt more complicated in reality than in theory. She knew that righteousness required persistence when faced with ambiguity.

She believed that staying faithful to her ethics would eventually guide her down the right path, even if it meant navigating through the territory. She would now observe and wait patiently for clarity to emerge from the shadows of uncertainty.

Chapter 8

Jaz slid into the worn vinyl booth across from Mia at their favorite corner diner. The mid-morning sun streamed through the windows, glinting off the chrome countertop.

"Hey, you," he said warmly, grasping her hand. "How are you holding up with everything going on?"

Mia smiled faintly, though her eyes betrayed lingering exhaustion and stress. "Oh, you know me. Hanging in there."

She took a sip of steaming coffee. "Honestly? The political pressure from higher-ups keeps mounting. But I refuse to back down."

Jaz nodded somberly, gently squeezing her hand. He admired her perseverance but worried about the toll this crusade was taking.

"Just promise me you'll take care of yourself. You can't pour from an empty cup," he said earnestly.

Mia sighed and then nodded. "I'll try. But only if you do the same." A hint of playful sternness entered her tone. "I know you carry the weight of everything on your shoulders."

Jaz chuckled softly. "Deal. We'll get each other through this the way we always have, together."

A comfortable silence settled between them, hands loosely intertwined on the tabletop. In this brief respite from their struggles, they drew strength from one another. Come what may, they would face the battles ahead side by side.

Mia managed a weary smile. "The police brass are still stonewalling the investigation into your dad's case at every turn. But I refuse to let it go."

She raised an eyebrow, her tone turning solemn. "Speaking of investigations, I heard you've been working closely with Alessandra lately. How's that going?"

Jaz hesitated, his expression pensive. "It's been a complicated partnership, to say the least. I'm trying to glean intel about the syndicate through her connections."

He lowered his voice. "But her shades-of-gray morality makes me uneasy sometimes. I have to walk a fine line."

Mia nodded, her eyes full of concern. "Just be careful, Jaz. Don't let her cunning manipulate you. Your intentions are good, but she can't be trusted."

"I'm staying cautious, believe me," Jaz assured, "but you're right to remind me she has her own agenda."

Eager to shift focus, he leaned forward. "Enough about me. Any promising developments on your end we should discuss?"

Mia lowered her voice, further ensuring privacy. "I've been investigating the police officer who took over your father's case when he went missing. There are warning signs in his past. I believe he intentionally obstructed the investigation of pursuing leads."

Jaz muttered under his breath in frustration. "This entire conspiracy just keeps expanding. We need to expose it." He anxiously tapped his fingers on the table before continuing." Let's have an honest conversation here. How are you holding up under all this pressure?"

Mia shook her head wryly and replied honestly, "To be frank? Sometimes, I have no idea; I need to make sure I do it right, not just for your dad but everyone else. It's just..." She paused, looking away.

Jaz gently placed his hand over hers. "What is it? You know you can confide in me, partner."

Reluctantly, Mia met his gaze. "I keep worrying that I've already made mistakes. Crossing boundaries in my pursuit of truth. But it troubles me deeply, you know? It feels like I'm betraying myself."

"Hey, your intentions are in the right place," Jaz reassured her. These things weigh on all of us. Together, we'll hold each other accountable and make things right."

Mia managed to smile. "Thank you. Just having someone standing by my side means more than you realize." She took out a folder from her bag and handed it to him. "Now take a look at this..."

Their dangerous yet just crusade continued, filled with doubts but fueled by their bond against corruption. As long as they stayed true to themselves and supported one another, the beacon of justice would ultimately triumph.

Chapter 9

Jaz was jolted awake by his cell phone ringing insistently. Bleary-eyed, he answered quickly.

"Uncle Jaz, it's me." Lisa's small and scared voice instantly alerted him.

Jaz sat bolt upright. "Lisa, what's wrong? Where are you?"

"I'm at the police station downtown. Can you get me, please? I screwed up bad." She sounded near tears.

"I'm on my way." Jaz was already out of bed and putting on clothes. "Are you hurt?"

"No, I'm okay; they're just holding me. Please hurry." Lisa hung up abruptly.

Jaz's pulse raced as he sped downtown. A million dire scenarios flashed through his mind. What trouble had his teenage niece gotten into now?

At the station, the officer at the desk directed him back to an interview room. Jaz burst in to find Lisa hunched over in a chair, looking small and scared.

Seeing her uncle, she leaped up and hugged him tightly. "I'm so sorry," she choked out.

Jaz stroked her hair. "Hey, hey, it's okay. Just tell me what happened."

They sat down across from each other. Lisa kept her eyes downcast as she explained, "Some friends and I were at a party, and things got crazy. People were doing drugs and drinking. I only had one beer, I swear!"

She looked up pleadingly. Jaz gestured for her to continue.

"The cops busted the party. A bunch of kids ran, but I got caught, and they brought me here." Fresh tears welled up. "I know I screwed up. Please don't tell Mom, she'll freak."

Jaz scrubbed a hand down his face, equal parts angry and relieved. "Lisa, you lied to me and broke the law. You could have gotten seriously hurt!"

Seeing her crestfallen expression, he softened. "But I'm not going to abandon you. I promised your dad I'd look out for you, and I will."

Lisa smiled small, gratefully. "I don't make it easy, but I'm really glad you're here."

Jaz rose and embraced his niece again. "Let's get you home." He knew they had painful conversations ahead. But the family came first, before vengeance for his father.

After dropping off a subdued Lisa at her mother's house, Jaz met Marcus and Mia at a cafe to update them. Both reacted with concern.

"That girl is starving for guidance," Marcus noted. "You may want to keep a closer eye on her for now."

Mia nodded, agreeing. "I know you want to investigate your dad's case, but Lisa needs you, too."

Jaz sighed heavily. "You're both right. I gotta strike a balance here somehow. She's acting out, but I hope I can get through to her."

Marcus smiled encouragingly. "If anyone can set her straight, it's you. Just lend that girl some wisdom and patience."

"Meanwhile, we'll keep surveilling our corrupt former boss," Mia added. "Could it be the break we need just around the corner?"

Jaz felt bolstered by having their support. Still, doubts lingered about his ability to juggle family and justice. He could only pray that this precarious balancing act would be held.

Over the next week, Jaz made more time for his niece, taking her to dinner and checking in more frequently. She remained sullen and abrupt at first. But slowly, their honest talks seemed to resonate.

One evening, over milkshakes, Lisa finally opened up and talked about her struggles. "With Dad gone, Mom working all the time...I know it's no excuse to act out. But I feel so alone sometimes like nobody cares or gets me."

Jaz's heart ached at her words. He had experienced that lost feeling all too well himself when his own father disappeared.

"I get it, believe me. When my dad vanished, I was angry and hurting, too," he admitted. "But people do care about you. I'm here whenever you need to talk, okay?"

Lisa nodded, appearing relieved someone understood. They parted with an embrace, and the gulf bridged at last. Jaz felt hopeful he could still steer his wounded niece towards the light.

Meanwhile, Mia finally got the chance to tail her corrupt former supervisor when he emerged from his seedy apartment. Keeping her distance, she tracked him to a rundown restaurant.

Slipping inside unseen, she observed him meeting with known syndicate affiliates. Gotcha, she thought. The proof of his criminal ties was now irrefutable.

But apprehending him herself was still too risky. She needed to take this evidence higher up the chain of command. But who could she trust? The lines between truth and complicity were hopelessly blurred.

After following the compromised cop to confirm he had no other suspicious stops, Mia headed home to decide her next move. She wished she could discuss it with Jaz, but he had his hands full getting his family in order.

Her thoughts were interrupted by her cell phone's ringing. Seeing it was Jaz, she answered quickly, "Hey, you. I was just thinking about you..."

Jaz sounded out of breath. "Mia, it's bad. Lisa got picked up and tried to steal a watch. She's being arrested."

"Oh no." Mia grabbed her keys and started moving. "Text me the precinct, and I'm on my way. We'll figure this out."

At the police station, Jaz was engulfed in a whirlwind of chaos as he argued fruitlessly with the desk sergeant. "Please, she's just a scared teenager who needs help, not jail!"

The stoic sergeant shook his head. "She committed a crime; we have to follow protocol."

As officers led a handcuffed Lisa away, she turned back, tears streaming down her face. "Uncle Jaz, please...I'm so sorry!"

Jaz's heart shattered when he saw his niece's anguished expression as she disappeared down the hall. He raked a hand through his hair in torment. How could this be happening?

Lisa's mom, Tasha, burst through the doors wild-eyed just then. "Jaz! What is going on? They just took my baby away in handcuffs!"

Jaz enveloped his distraught sister in a fierce hug as she broke down sobbing. "Shh shh, I've got you. Lisa made a mistake, but we'll get her through this."

Tasha pulled back, mascara streaking her cheeks. "But juvenile detention? For how long? I can't lose my daughter!" Her voice climbed hysterically.

Jaz grasped her shoulders. "Listen to me. Lisa has our unconditional love and support. This is just a stumble, not her whole path."

Tasha trembled, grappling to accept her daughter's devastating misstep. "I just wish I understood why...we tried hard to set her right."

Jaz hugged Tasha again, his own heart heavy. "I know. But sometimes life leads us down unexpected detours. What matters is we never abandon hope."

Mia approached cautiously, her eyes brimming with compassion. "Jaz is right. With our help, Lisa will get through this."

Tasha managed a slight, tearful nod. "Having you both here means everything. I can't lose faith now when my daughter needs it most."

At the courthouse for Lisa's hearing, Jaz and Tasha waited anxiously for Lisa's hearing to be called.

Mia slipped in and sat next to Jaz. "Do you have any updates on reducing the charges?" he asked.

Mia smiled. "I had a conversation with the ADA and highlighted Lisa's family and upbringing. I also shared some insights regarding corruption within the department. It convinced him to consider leniency."

Jaz raised his eyebrows in surprise. "How did you manage that?"

"I have my methods, "Mia replied playfully. "Let's just say those in power would prefer to handle this than create a public spectacle."

"Mia, I'm at a loss for words. Thank you." Jaz tightly embraced her. Thanks to her move, Lisa would likely face probation instead of imprisonment.

During the hearing, the judge agreed to probation and community service with the condition that Lisa attend counseling sessions. Jaz and Tasha assured him that they would diligently comply with all requirements.

As Lisa was escorted out of the courtroom, she silently said "thank you" to Mia. Jaz turned to his friend, his gratitude evident in his eyes.

"I can't believe you took such a risk for my family. Lisa is getting another chance because of you." His voice choked with emotion.

Mia brushed it off. "Your dad put himself on the line to bring down criminals. It's only fair that I follow his example for his loved ones." She playfully nudged his shoulder. "Besides, that's what partners are for."

That evening, during dinner, Jaz said to Lisa, "I know it hasn't been easy for you. If you embrace this, I believe it will steer you in the right direction.

Lisa nodded, her demeanor subdued. "I apologize sincerely for my mistakes. I am determined to improve my life and make you and Mom proud of me. I truly value what Mia did for me today. I will not squander this opportunity."

Jaz smiled warmly, a renewed sense of hope shining through. "You possess the potential to make an impact in this world. Believe in yourself. Remember that you're not alone on this journey. We're here by your side."

They conversed into the evening, working toward rebuilding their bond. Although challenges lay ahead, Jaz felt confident that Lisa had made a breakthrough. Their family's unwavering commitment to finding redemption amidst darkness would guide them toward a future.

Chapter 10

The rain fell in persistent sheets as Mia parked down the street from the seedy apartment building. Despite the punishing deluge, she kept a vigilant watch for her target—her corrupt former police supervisor, whom she suspected was complicit in the cover-up surrounding Jaz's father's case.

Mia's fingers drummed anxiously on the steering wheel as the wipers swished back and forth. She knew this stakeout was risky business—if her bosses got wind of the fact that she was investigating a veteran officer without authorization, it could cost her badge. But the rotten stench of buried truth compelled her to action, no matter the risk.

Finally, her patience was rewarded when a bulky, disheveled figure emerged from the apartment lobby: John Mahoney, the former lead detective on Jaz's dad's case before his suspicious removal.

Following him across town. Mia watched from her car as he stood outside a seedy storefront. Snapping photos of her corrupt former supervisor consorting with criminals. Gotcha, she thought with grim satisfaction. This brazen criminality couldn't be ignored any longer.

Taking a deep breath, she called dispatch. "This is Detective Sanchez. I have eyes on a former police lieutenant engaged in racketeering and corruption. I request immediate backup."

Within minutes, two patrol cars screeched up. Mia identified herself and directed them to make the arrest. As they hauled the stunned crooked cop away, Mia knew blowback was coming. But the price of justice was worth paying.

The Chief's face purpled with rage as Mia laid out the incriminating photos. "This is outrageous, Sanchez! You had no clearance for surveillance on a veteran detective."

Mia stood her ground. "With all due respect, sir, the corruption speaks for itself. We have a duty to investigate"

"Enough!" The Chief cut her off sharply. "Turn in your badge and gun. You're suspended pending a formal review if you're lucky."

Fuming but resolute, Mia surrendered her shield and weapon. She had expected resistance, but the truth mattered above all else. She could weather this storm.

Exiting the station, Mia blinked back furious tears as the doomsday words "suspended" and "review" echoed in her mind. Had her zeal backfired? Was she losing perspective in this crusade?

Before despair could take root, her phone buzzed. "Mia, it's Jaz. I've been trying to reach you. We need to meet tonight. It's urgent."

Relief flooded through Mia at the comforting sound of his voice. If anyone could understand and ground her, it would be Jaz. They needed each other now more than ever.

Jaz sat in his study scrutinizing the coded journal of a syndicate informant he had managed to obtain through back channels. Most of it was still indecipherable, but specific phrases hinted at high-level police complicity in his father's murder.

Hours later, Jaz welcomed Mia inside, embracing her tightly. "It's so damn good to see you." At his kitchen table, he unraveled the convoluted threads that hinted at internal corruption sabotaging the case.

Mia smacked the table angrily. "I knew it! That's why that slimeball Mahoney conveniently got reassigned." She took a deep breath. "Which means this goes even deeper than we realized. We've got to be smart."

Jaz nodded solemnly; the stakes were now agonizingly clear. Powerful enemies surrounded them, wearing familiar, trusted faces. Their allegiance to truth was being put to the ultimate test.

The next day, Jaz stopped by Alessandra's law office, hoping to glean information from her syndicate connections. But her receptionist said she had abruptly taken a leave of absence for 'personal reasons'. Unease prickled his spine. What was she up to?

Meanwhile, Alessandra pored through boxes of cold case files in her temporary basement office. She had requested obscure cases, searching for intersections with Jaz's father. Hour nine of the mind-numbing task was approaching when a detail in a dusty file suddenly made her sit bolt upright.

The suspect in this decades-old unsolved murder was last seen meeting with a man matching the description of Jaz's father. Alessandra's pulse raced. This couldn't be a coincidence. What had he stumbled into?

That night, Alessandra gathered Jaz, Mia, and Marcus at Magnolia Plantation, a sprawling estate fronted by elegant white columns and draped by Spanish moss. As they walked the torch-lit gardens, she urgently explained her discovery's connection to Jaz's dad.

"This changes everything," Mia said breathlessly. "It's not just the syndicate. Your father must have unearthed something even bigger."

Marcus looked grave. "I did some more digging. There are people inside the department protecting external interests."

Jaz felt the gravity of their mission deepening. Layers of deception still hid truths that had cost his father's life. "Then we keep digging until we expose every damn lie."

Alessandra's phone suddenly rang. Her face paled as she answered. Her hand trembled as she showed them the unknown caller's chilling text message: "Beware shadows bearing gifts. The price of truth is eternal."

Marcus' forehead creased with concern. "This proves we're on the right track if mysterious forces try to silence us with threats."

"Agreed, we can't let faceless cowards intimidate us," Mia said firmly.

Jaz nodded, his jaw clenched with determination. "Now we just have to decipher what 'shadows bearing gifts' could symbolize."

They brainstormed possibilities as they continued along the walking paths, lined by ancient oak trees draped in wispy Spanish moss. The tranquil beauty of the plantation grounds contrasted starkly with their rising unease.

"Maybe it refers to someone we think is an ally but has deceived us," Marcus suggested.

Mia chewed her lip. "We also need to look at existing evidence through fresh eyes. We may have missed something."

The faint glow of fireflies danced around them as dusk deepened, mirroring the sparks of revelation flickering in their minds. They were unraveling secrets that powerful forces clearly wanted to keep buried, and the stakes grew ever higher.

After leaving the plantation grounds, Jaz sat alone in his apartment, looking through old family photos, his father's smiling face shining up at him. "What were you trying to expose that got you killed?" he murmured. "Give me a sign here."

He opened the journal again, scrutinizing each cryptic phrase under a magnifying glass. Most still made no sense, but a hidden pattern was emerging...

At home, Mia looked through the dusty boxes she had managed to sneak out of Jaz's father's cold case files again, looking for any connection with his disappearance. Around 3 AM, tired but caffeinated, she discovered a receipt with a partial credit card number.

They gathered again at sunrise at Jaz's house to share revelations. Mia showed the receipt linking cases. Jaz revealed coded journal patterns suggesting police complicity.

"This proves my father uncovered something threatening powerful figures," Jaz said excitedly. "We're getting close to the truth!"

Mia flipped through pages eagerly but then halted. "Wait...what if this is still misdirection? We can't fully trust any 'evidence' yet."

Jaz hesitated, realizing she had a point. "You're right. We need to be strategic. Get concrete proof that is not easily fabricated."

"I may have an idea about that," Alessandra suddenly piped up. Intrigued, they turned to her, and the flames within reflected in her eyes.

"A client of mine who flipped is privy to the syndicate's deepest secrets. I think I can persuade him to talk."

Jaz raised an eyebrow. "And how do you plan on 'persuading' him?"

"Leave that to me," Alessandra replied cryptically. "Let's just say I can be very convincing when necessary."

Their path ahead was still murky, but one thing was clear - they were united against the shadows and determined to illuminate the truth no matter the cost. With loyalty, tenacity, and faith in each other, they would prevail.

After leaving Jaz's house close to midnight, Mia decided to drive by Mahoney's seedy place again, feeling sure he was the rotten apple spoiling the whole barrel. Parking down the block, she watched the building's entrance from her inconspicuous sedan.

Around 2 AM, a bulky figure emerged, back hunched against the rain. Mia's breath caught - it was Mahoney. She stealthily pursued his car through the nearly deserted predawn streets, hanging back to avoid detection.

Mahoney led her to an isolated stretch of riverbank lining the Cooper River. Parking near a decaying warehouse, he disappeared inside. Mia carefully approached the same door to listen.

She could just make out Mahoney's gravelly voice. "The heat is on with that case. We gotta accelerate the plan."

Mia strained to hear the muffled reply. "Take care of Blackwell and the girl. I'll handle the D.A."

A cold fist of fear clenched Mia's heart. They were all targets now, but Jaz and Lisa's lives were in jeopardy. She had to warn them before it was too late.

Later that day, at the Department of Corrections, Jaz and Alessandra anxiously awaited the prisoner's arrival. Jaz nervously bounced his leg under the metal table, unable to contain his pent-up anticipation. This shadowy insider was their best chance of obtaining the crucial evidence to expose the syndicate's secrets. It might provide the missing puzzle piece to unravel the web of lies and corruption if they could persuade him to talk. The minutes stretched on until the door unexpectedly opened. Jaz sat up straighter, pulse quickening. This mysterious figure potentially held the power to unlock mysteries that had eluded justice for decades.

The guards escorted a handcuffed Vince DeLuca into the stark interrogation room. His cold eyes briefly sized up Jaz and Alessandra before he sat down across from them, leaning back casually.

Alessandra fixed DeLuca with an icy stare. "Well, if it isn't Vince DeLuca. I expected better cooperation from you after all I've done to help with your legal situation."

DeLuca shrugged, unmoved. "Sorry, Counselor, but I've got nothing to share today. My secrets stay buried."

Jaz studied DeLuca intently, sensing there was more below the surface. He wondered what leverage Alessandra had over this steely inmate.

Alessandra leaned forward, her voice dropping to a whisper. "If you care about your family on the outside, you'll rethink your position."

DeLuca's confident façade wavered slightly at the mention of his family, but he kept up the bluff. "You got nothing on me. I walk out of here in one piece either way."

Jaz saw the flash of fear in DeLuca's eyes before his nonchalant mask slipped back into place. There was a weakness here they could exploit. He caught Alessandra's eye and gave her an almost imperceptible nod to keep pressing.

"Tell us what you know about who was behind Detective Blackwell's murder," Alessandra continued. "Share the truth, and I can make certain...inconsistencies in your case disappear."

DeLuca licked his lips nervously, a sheen of sweat on his brow. "My secrets die with me, understand? Talking won't fix anything." But his false bravado was crumbling.

Alessandra leaned in closer, her voice dropping to a hushed tone. "I'm aware of your son, with Carla Ricci, the one you've kept hidden from your wife for 14 years. If you want to keep his secret intact, you'll provide us with the information we seek."

DeLucas's expression turned into a mask of fear, his face losing its color as if all blood had drained away. A faint layer of sweat formed on his forehead as he comprehended the chilling implications of Alessandra's threat. His guarded secrets, built over decades, now hung precariously on the edge, ready to unravel and expose his double life.

DeLuca surged against his cuffs, his face twisting in rage. "You heartless snake! That was a cheap shot, and you know it!"

Unfazed by DeLucas' outburst, Alessandra maintained her intense gaze upon him with piercing green eyes. "Start talking. I will make one call to bring down your fragile house of cards."

DeLuca slumped back in defeat, completely broken, and any remnants of resistance faded away like a candle being extinguished. When he finally spoke again, his voice trembled with haunting desperation.

"Alright, damn it! I'll tell you what I know." DeLuca snarled.

Jaz and Alessandra exchanged a satisfied look as she gave him a pen and pad. She then called for a uniformed officer to set up a recorder.

"Start from the beginning," Jaz said, steel in his voice. "And leave nothing out."

DeLuca nervously licked his thin lips again, his eyes darting around. Finally, in a gravelly whisper, he began unraveling the secrets that had cost Jaz's father his life decades ago.

"It goes all the way to the top - the mayor, the chief of police, even a few judges on the payroll. They've been running this racket for over 30 years."

He revealed how Mayor Edwin Richardson took bribes from real estate developers to push out low-income families in favor of lucrative high-rise condos. Police Chief Raymond Reynolds used civil forfeiture laws to seize assets from anyone who dared challenge city hall, keeping a cut for himself. Judge Lawrence Pritchard accepted suitcases of cash to make incriminating evidence disappear for syndicate members.

The syndicate formed over thirty years ago when Richardson and his close allies realized they could profit tremendously from their positions of power. At first, it was just skimming city contracts and grafting from local businesses. But as greed took hold, the operation grew more complex and ruthless.

They brought the chief of police into the fold early on, knowing they would need the force under their control. With Reynolds able to stall or shut down any criminal investigations, the syndicate operated with impunity, branching out into money laundering, extortion, and eventually narcotics and arms trafficking. The vast profits allowed them to bribe more officials and expand their malignant influence.

Anyone who posed a threat soon found their reputation or livelihood destroyed by the syndicate's reach. Or, in the case of Jaz's father, they were silenced permanently. The damaging revelations shed light on decades of corruption, lies, and murder perpetrated to maintain power.

Jaz's blood ran cold, listening to the ruinous depths of the depravity. These were men sworn to serve the public good, now exposed as soulless criminals who abused their authority without remorse. But the dark secrets were coming to light at last.

Chapter 11

Armed with DeLuca's damning confession, Jaz rushed to meet Mia and Marcus at O'Malley's Pub. Inside, they sat in a quiet booth near the rear entrance. Mia hurriedly explained, overhearing Mahoney and unknown figures plotting to "take care" of Jaz and Lisa.

Jaz felt his blood turn to ice water. "Lisa's in immediate danger. We must get to her right now!"

"I'm coming with you," Mia declared, checking her weapon. "We'll keep her safe."

Marcus urged caution. "This could be exactly what they want - to draw you two out in the open." He turned to Mia. "We need to strategize this carefully."

"There's no time!" Jaz exploded. "Lisa needs us NOW!" He headed for the door.

Mia blocked his path. "Marcus is right. We can't react rashly, or we're all dead." Her eyes pleaded with him. "We get one shot at this."

Jaz raked a hand through his hair, knowing they spoke the truth but tormented about leaving Lisa vulnerable. "You're both right...okay, what's the smart play here?"

They rapidly discussed contingencies for safely extracting Lisa to a remote location. Jaz was only half-listening, consumed with worry. Please, God, keep her safe, he prayed desperately.

After agreeing on a plan, Jaz and Mia raced to Tasha's house. It was ominously dark, and no one answered their frantic knocks. Drawing their weapons, they forced their way inside.

"Tasha? Lisa?" Jaz cried out, to no response besides the echo of his own voice. The house was empty. They were too late.

Rushing into Lisa's bedroom, Jaz spotted a piece of notepaper on her unmade bed. With dread constricting his chest, he picked it up.

The menacing message was short: "If you want to see them again, come to 712 Ocean Avenue at midnight. Alone."

Jaz's hands trembled, nearly dropping the ominously brief note. Coming here alone at midnight was undoubtedly a trap, but what choice did he have? Lisa and Tasha's lives hung in the balance.

Jaz met Mia's worried gaze with steely resolve. "I'm going. And I'm getting them out, whatever it takes."

Mia gripped his arm. "We're in this together, Jaz. I'll be right there with you."

Jaz hesitated, visions of her being used against him flashing through his mind. But he realized arguing was futile - Mia's loyalty was unconditional.

As midnight approached, they took up strategic positions blocks away from the grimy abandoned cannery at 712 Ocean Avenue. Their weapons were locked and loaded for the coming confrontation.

Jaz approached the front entrance warily. The creaking door yielded to darkness. He gripped his gun tightly and swept his flashlight beam over gnarled pipes and rusted chains.

"Tasha? Lisa?" His urgent whisper echoed eerily through the vast emptiness. Where were they?

Suddenly, blinding floodlights switched on, searing Jaz's eyes. He raised his hand to shield his face. His pulse roared in his ears.

A cruel voice rang out from the shadows. "Welcome, Pastor. We've been expecting you." Rough hands seized Jaz, wrenching away his weapon.

As his vision adjusted, Jaz spotted two armed thugs flanking a bound and gagged Tasha and Lisa. Red-hot rage flooded through him.

"Let them go, you worthless scum! They're innocent." Jaz struggled uselessly against his captors' viselike grip.

The syndicate boss emerged from the shadows, smiling coldly. "Now, now, let's talk civilly. You have something we need - the confession."

Jaz spat defiantly. "Go to hell! You'll never lay hands on it."

The boss nodded to one of the thugs, who delivered a vicious blow to Tasha's stomach. She cried out through the gag.

"Stop!" Jaz shouted desperately. "I swear you'll pay for touching them." Impotent fury coursed through him.

The boss leaned in menacingly. "The price is high for stubbornness. Perhaps the girl needs persuading, too."

Lisa's muffled screams pierced Jaz as she was backhanded brutally across the face. "Okay, stop!" he cried, sagging in defeat. "I'll take you to the confession. Just please, don't hurt them anymore."

The boss grinned sadistically. "See? Now we can have a productive conversation." He gestured for Jaz to be released. "Take us to the documents."

Steeling himself, Jaz led the armed caravan towards Marcus' townhouse, where the confession was hidden, desperately stalling for an idea.

Once Mia realized where they were headed, she took a different route and beat them there. She parked in the rear, quickly gathered her weapons, and ran up the fire escape of the four-story brownstone. Now lying prone, she tracked them through the RPG's sights, her finger resting beside the trigger. She inhaled slowly, her mind blank and focused.

Jaz's eyes darted rapidly as they turned down Maple Street, knowing Mia would be shadowing them. Suddenly, he spotted her stealthily positioned on a nearby rooftop, RPG launcher braced on her shoulder as she aimed.

The lead SUV crossed into her field of fire. Exhaling calmly, Mia squeezed the trigger. The RPG roared as it streaked downwards in a trail of smoke.

With sudden explosive force, the syndicate vehicle flipped and careened under Mia's expertly aimed rocket-propelled grenade assault. Flames erupted as the SUVs smashed and rolled violently.

In the chaos, Jaz tackled Lisa and Tasha to the floor, shielding their bodies protectively as heat washed over them. Shouts and cries rang out from the wreckage. Jaz managed to free the side door, and they escaped the burning vehicle.

Mia fired again, striking the other vehicle broadside. As dazed gunmen stumbled from the overturned, burning SUVs, she rained down merciless sniper fire from her rooftop vantage point.

Within minutes, the street was silent again except for the crackle of flames. Mia secured her weapon and raced down the fire escape to rendezvous with Jaz.

Her bold surprise attack had given her the advantage they desperately needed. Catching the enemy off guard, even for a moment, would change the entire battle. Mia rushed over to check for injuries as Jaz untied his sobbing but unharmed sister and niece. "You're both safe now. It's over," he soothed, embracing them tightly.

Mia offered Jaz a brief, fierce smile, knowing the fight continued. But with her partner beside her, she was ready for anything.

Lisa looked up at Mia in awe. "You took them all out...that was incredible!" Despite the circumstances, Mia had to laugh. Lisa was a resilient kid.

With the syndicate decimated and the damning confession in hand, they finally had justice for Jaz's father within reach. Mia had repeatedly proven the lengths she would go to protect her new family. United and unbreakable, they were unstoppable.

In the aftermath, Jaz insisted Lisa and Tasha be placed under armed protection at an undisclosed safe house until things calmed down. Despite their protests, he refused to compromise their safety.

"We made so many sacrifices to take down the syndicate. I won't risk you now," Jaz said, fiercely embracing them. They relented, moved by his profound protective devotion.

With his family secure, Jaz met Mia and Marcus at his home to strategize their final moves. Mia was still wired from the intense shootout.

"We need to go on the offensive before they regroup," she urged, pacing like a caged lioness. "We take the fight right to their doorstep for once."

Marcus gently cautioned restraint. "This confession gives us power. We need to be smart about using it for maximum impact." He turned to Jaz. "No emotion. Only cold strategy."

Jaz nodded thoughtfully. "You're right, my friend. I want to blast this story from the rooftops, but we get one shot to expose the rot at the core."

Mia exhaled, acknowledging the wisdom in patience. "Okay, we do this right. Take our time lining up the dominoes before we start toppling them."

United in renewed purpose, they got to work strategically disseminating snippets from the explosive confession to light fires under the feet of the corrupt officials it implicated. Marcus and Mia kept digging for even more skeletons in closets. The foundations of lies quaked beneath their assault.

In his study, Jaz looked up from his Bible at the photos of his father lining the shelves. "We're so close now, Dad," he whispered. "Your sacrifice won't be in vain much longer." Though the past could never be changed, finally, the future showed glimmers of hope.

Chapter 12

In the weeks following the dissemination of the damning confession, the foundations of lies and corruption trembled as public outrage grew. Every day brought new revelations as journalists relentlessly pursued threads implicating officials at the highest levels.

Under intense scrutiny, many architects of the criminal syndicate scrambled to cover their tracks and distance themselves from the fallout. But the light now shining in the shadows revealed the rot they could no longer conceal.

At City Hall, Mayor Edwin Richardson found himself besieged on all sides by reporters demanding answers about leaked documents tying him to lucrative kickback schemes. Dabbing sweat from his brow, he dodged their shouted questions while fighting his way to the idling town car outside. This house of cards was crumbling fast.

From the back of the press scrum, Jaz observed the mayor's downfall with grim satisfaction. Flashing blue and red lights signaled the arrival of federal authorities, finally empowered to follow the evidence wherever it led. Richardson could no longer stonewall.

Across town, Chief of Police Raymond Reynolds emerged scowling from his home to address the gathered media. "The allegations against this department are outrageous and false," he blustered into the microphone. But his voice lacked its usual intimidating command.

Mia watched the statement from her car down the block, a predatory glint in her eye. The defensive chief was already marked prey. After years of complicity and coverups, he would finally face justice. She would make sure of it.

At the FBI field office, Marcus provided inside guidance as agents poured over records subpoenaed regarding judges accepting bribes to make cases disappear. One prominent judge swiftly submitted his resignation to avoid charges. The untouchables were proving mortal after all.

From the relative safety of their undisclosed location, Tasha and Lisa watched the stunning developments on the news. "They really did it—they took down the bad guys," Lisa marveled. Tasha silently offered prayers of gratitude for her brother's safety.

A week later, Jaz and Mia walked up the marble courthouse steps as Mayor Richardson arrived for his arraignment in handcuffs, head bowed before the blindfolded statue of justice. Mia clasped Jaz's hand tightly, sensing his roiling emotions.

"This is just the beginning - the ripples will spread further," she assured him in an undertone. Jaz managed a terse nod, heart pounding as decades of secrets unraveled before him. Whatever came next, Mia would be there, his pillar of strength.

In a hastily called press conference the next day, Police Chief Reynolds announced his resignation while denying personal wrongdoing. Eyes hard, he proclaimed his intention to focus on clearing his name of "false accusations."

Watching Reynolds' defiant speech on the precinct TV, Mia snorted derisively. "Guy just can't admit when he's beaten." She turned to smirk at Jaz. "Of course, we know how this ends for him." Jaz chuckled in agreement. Unhumbled villains often had further yet to fall.

At sundown, Jaz joined Marcus overlooking the city skyline from the steeple of an old stone cathedral. His friend turned with an uncharacteristically somber expression. "I know your soul still seeks justice for your father's murder. But you tread dangerous ground now, my brother. Are you prepared?"

Jaz closed his eyes as the last crimson rays faded below the horizon. "I've walked in shadows long enough. Whatever comes, I face it without fear." Opening his eyes, he embraced Marcus fiercely before heading home with renewed purpose.

Over the ensuing month, the investigation expanded rapidly as panicked suspects implicated higher-ups in exchange for leniency. Even Judge Lawrence Pritchard resigned quietly rather than fight allegations of judicial corruption. The house of cards collapsed inward, the foundation crumbling.

On a sunny June morning, Mia stopped by Jaz's community garden, smiling to see children laughing while they planted flowers. Her reverie was interrupted by an urgent call – after months of evading capture, former Chief Reynolds had been arrested attempting to flee the country. Mia allowed herself a fierce grin of satisfaction. The hunted had become prey.

Late that night, Jaz kept vigil in his study, poring over case files surrounded by photos of happier times. He still ached for justice denied 30 years ago. But the long-awaited turning tide buoyed his weary spirit.

"We finally broke through, Dad," he whispered. "Your sacrifice tore holes in their cloak of darkness. Now we rip it away for good." Setting down a photo of his beaming father, Jaz finally headed off to sleep, a heart lighter than it had been in decades.

The following day dawned clear and warm as Mia approached Jaz's house. He greeted her with a rare, unburdened smile. "Reynolds is to be transferred to the federal lockup today," she reported. "I have contacts on transport security who will ensure he gets there without incident. Then we have him right where we want him."

Jaz clapped her shoulder warmly. "Your perseverance through all this has been such a gift. Couldn't have done this without you." He held her gaze with heartfelt sincerity.

Mia brushed off the praise, but her eyes glistened. "We make a pretty great team," she admitted. Impulsively, she pulled Jaz into a fierce embrace under the summer sun. Together, they were changing what many had believed unchangeable.

In the following weeks, the breadth of the corruption probe multiplied as sympathetic judges signed off on wiretaps and subpoenas. Numerous backroom deals and secret payouts surfaced, sending shockwaves through the city's monied elite. Everyone was now fair game in this relentless crusade for truth.

Marcus gathered Jaz and Mia in the garden behind his brownstone on a muggy July night. In hushed tones, he confirmed federal racketeering indictments were imminent against Mayor Richardson, Chief Reynolds, and several prominent businessmen linked to the criminal syndicate.

"It's unraveling now - they're turning on each other to get plea deals," Marcus revealed. "We're close to exposing the rotten core for good." He raised his glass in a wordless toast, pride and hope shining in his eyes. Mia and Jaz joined the salute, spirits soaring.

One golden summer evening, Jaz lingered in the community garden after volunteers had left, surveying the flourishing rows of vegetables and flowers. Children's joyous laughter echoed down the rows as the fading light washed the garden in hazy amber.

Jaz closed his eyes, letting the gentle breeze wash over his face. "Your hope lives on, Dad," he whispered. "We're healing this city, block by block. Gathering light to drive away the shadows."

Opening his eyes with a deep breath, Jaz felt ready for the challenging road still ahead. For the first time, real justice finally seemed possible. And where justice dwelled, no darkness could endure. Jaz would see this through—for his father, for those who walked this path with him, and for the future still unfolding.

Chapter 13

The magnificent colors from the stained-glass windows filled Spirit Song Fellowship as Jaz stood at the carved oak pulpit. Looking out at the faces in the pews, he felt a deep connection to this community that had supported him through thick and thin. Now, with justice served and shadows dispersed, he was ready to share a message of renewed hope.

"My friends, we have faced tough times together," Jaz began, his voice filled with warmth and conviction.

"When hope seemed lost, and corruption had taken root, we refused to give in to despair. Through our unwavering faith and commitment to what's right, we brought the deeds into the light."

A murmur of agreement rippled through the congregation. Each person there had experienced firsthand the oppression imposed by merciless individuals, but those days were now behind them.

"We encountered challenges and made sacrifices along this journey," Jaz acknowledged, his movements animated as he paced on the stage. Our bodies may bear scars from battles fought, but every struggle was worth it. By exposing the web of lies surrounding us, we found redemption flowing in."

Jaz's gaze met Mia's and Marcus' as they sat in the front row. Their loyalty and courage played a role in this victory, which would not have been possible without them. In response, they exchanged nods filled with emotion.

"However, our work doesn't stop at this point," cautioned Jaz, his voice filled with conviction. "There are still lingering shadows in our community. We can push them back if we unite and show unwavering compassion and dedication to justice."

Jaz drew inspiration from Amos 5:24. Passionately recited, "But let judgment run down as waters, and righteousness as a mighty stream.' These words will rejuvenate the soul of our city!"

Engrossed congregants leaned forward, some with tears welling up as Jaz's message deeply resonated within their hearts. They had long yearned for justice. Now, finally, the tides were turning.

"Take heart, my people!" thundered Jaz as he tightly held onto the edges of the pulpit. "The light has pierced through! Don't accept cruelty and corruption as inevitable anymore. You have discovered your ability to bring light into the darkness!"

To conclude, he invited anyone seeking solace or guidance to the altar. Many knelt at the carved wooden rail, seeking guidance after enduring prolonged hardships. With compassion, Jaz ministered to everyone, providing the wisdom and comfort their spirits longed.

Observing his worn-out community, finding solace within these walls, Jaz offered a prayer of gratitude.

Their shared hardships culminated in earned redemption under the guiding light of righteousness. However, the eternal struggle between good and evil remained unabated despite injustice.

Following the service, Jaz warmly greeted each departing individual, exchanging embraces. When Mia and Marcus approached, he tightly embraced them. "We confronted an adversary and emerged triumphant," Jaz said solemnly.

Marcus firmly grasped his shoulder. "Because we stayed united in our purpose. To uphold truth and justice." Mia's eyes welled up with tears. "No matter how challenging the path is, we walk it together. Let's never forget that."

In the weeks following, activists and reformers exerted pressure that began yielding positive results. Acting Mayor Ross implemented measures to oversee city contracts and finances. Neighborhood committees were formed to advocate for resource distribution.

With the upcoming election approaching, many encouraged Jaz to run for city council to solidify the change he had helped initiate. After considering this, he concluded that his talents would be better utilized outside politics.

"I'm truly honored by the support, but I feel my true calling lies here serving this community," he told his allies during a gathering. "Nevertheless, I will stand alongside anyone willing to embark on the path of public service."

While they were disappointed, they understood his decision. Jaz always prioritized nurturing community roots. He aimed to empower a generation of leaders while advocating for those without a voice.

A year after the regime's downfall, the city unveiled a bronze memorial honoring those who sacrificed everything to expose the truth. Jaz delivered a speech representing his father and others who were being commemorated.

"May this monument symbolize our restored faith in justice," declared Jaz with conviction in his voice. "May we never forget the sacrifices made by those who walked through the fire so the truth can ultimately prevail."

Marcus and Mia stood next to Jaz as he traced his father's name engraved on the marker. "Your legacy lives on, Dad," he whispered. The soft summer breeze seemed to respond.

That night, Mia joined Jaz for a candlelight memorial. She linked her arm through his. "Your dad would be incredibly proud of the person you've become," Mia said, her eyes shimmering with emotion.

Jaz pulled her close under the sky, enveloping her in an embrace. "I can only keep going because of you. Your presence gives me the strength I need."

Mia rested her head on his shoulder. "We've faced hardships together. Long as we stand side by side, I believe we can overcome anything."

Jaz kissed her head, his heart overflowing with love and gratitude. The flames ignited hope, redemption, and justice, burning brightly against the darkness. Together, they vowed to nurture that flame of any challenges that lay ahead.

In the following months, winds of change swept through the city, dispersing every trace of corruption left by the regime.

The End.

Don't miss out!

Visit the website below and you can sign up to receive emails whenever Odell Theadford publishes a new book. There's no charge and no obligation.

https://books2read.com/r/B-A-CPDZ-JDYPC

BOOKS 2 READ

Connecting independent readers to independent writers.